What to Do
on a
DRAGON DAY

What to Do
on a
DRAGON DAY

AND OTHER FRIENDSHIP STORIES
Compiled by the Editors
of
Highlights for Children

Compilation copyright © 1995 by Highlights for Children, Inc.
Contents copyright by Highlights for Children, Inc.
Published by Highlights for Children, Inc.
P.O. Box 18201
Columbus, Ohio 43218-0201
Printed in the United States of America

ISBN 0-87534-637-5

Highlights is a registered trademark of Highlights for Children, Inc.

CONTENTS

What to Do on a DRAGON DAY

By Marilyn Kratz

"What a dragon day this was, Mom," grumbled Adam. He plopped his book bag onto the table and headed for the refrigerator. "I forgot to study for my spelling test, my shoelace broke, and Joey kicked my soccer ball onto the roof of the school building at recess."

"I'm dragging, too," said Mom with a sigh. "The baby has been fussy all day, and I just burned the bread crumbs for the top of the casserole."

"Oh, no!" groaned Adam. "The crumbs are my favorite part. And I see we're out of milk."

7

Adam closed the refrigerator a little harder than necessary, grabbed an orange, and went out to sit on the front porch steps. Next door, Adam's friend Holly was jumping rope.

"Ninety-eight, ninety-nine, one hundred. Hi, Adam!" She jumped over and sat down beside him. "You look grumpy. What's wrong?"

"Everything's going wrong today," said Adam. He broke a piece off the orange and offered it to Holly.

"Thanks," said Holly. She ate the piece of orange silently. Then she said, "So what are you going to do about it?"

"What can I do?" asked Adam. "Some days just make me feel like a grumpy dragon, and today's one of them."

"Well, there must be something you can do to feel better," insisted Holly.

"What do you want me to do—make a list?" huffed Adam.

"Great idea!" said Holly, jumping up. "Wait here."

She ran to her house and returned with a pencil and notepad.

"What's that for?" asked Adam.

"For the list," said Holly. "We can make a list of all the things you could do to feel better."

"That's a silly idea," grumbled Adam.

"Well, do you have a better one?" asked Holly.

"Nope."

"Come on, then." She wrote the number *1* on her pad.

For a minute Adam just sat there and frowned. Then Holly began to write beside the number.

"Drink a glass of lemonade," Adam read from the pad. "Well, I do like lemonade. That might help."

"We're on our way!" declared Holly with a grin. "Now, you think of one."

"Hmmm," Adam thought for a while. "Taking a shower might help wash the grumps away."

Holly added that to the list.

"I'm going to put 'read a book' next," she decided.

Adam suggested, "Think about the best spelling grade you ever got."

"Help Mom bake cookies," was Holly's next idea.

Their ideas started coming so fast that Holly hardly had time to write them down as they called them out.

"Play soccer with Dad."

"Do ten cartwheels."

"Make a picture for your grandma."

"Pound a nail in a board."

"Hug your favorite teddy bear."

They began to giggle as they thought of funny ideas to add to the list.

"Read all your T-shirts backward."

"Sneak up on your sneakers."

"Write a letter to a Martian."

"Start a collection of real rainbows."

"Make hats for earthworms."

"Tickle a chicken with a feather."

By that time, they were both laughing out loud.

"It worked!" shouted Adam.

"What worked?" asked Holly.

"This list!" declared Adam. "I'm not feeling grumpy anymore."

"Great!" said Holly. "Here. You'd better keep this list."

"Thanks," said Adam. "But I have to add one more. It's the best way to get rid of a dragon day."

Holly watched Adam write. Then they both laughed. "That is the best one," she said. Holly read Adam's idea out loud. "Make a list with a friend."

A House of their Own

By Carolyn Bowman

Mrs. Terwiggle loved her new home in the country. She loved the birds who sang in the trees. She loved the flowers that grew in her garden. She loved the children who lived next door. She loved the wide blue sky and all the sunshine. She even loved rainy days, because rain washed everything clean. Having everything clean was very important to Mrs. Terwiggle.

She kept her house spit-spot tidy, right down to the doorknobs. So imagine how she felt about mice! "They don't belong inside," Mrs. Terwiggle would say. "They make such a mess."

If ever she saw a mouse, her hair would stand on end. Her arms would hang like beef steaks. Her lips would quiver, and she would scream, "Out! Get out!"

Now this was a problem, because Mrs. Terwiggle was up to her eyeballs in mice.

At first she didn't notice, for mice are small and secret creatures. One mouse came. And then another. Two more came, and then their brothers. Next came the aunt mice and uncle mice and cousin mice. Then came the sister mice, who made the mistake of showing themselves to Mrs. Terwiggle.

"Out! Get out!"

They did. For a while.

Mrs. Terwiggle went back to watching the birds, the flowers, the children, the blue sky, and the sunshine. And, one by one, the mice returned.

They slept in the attic. They played in the walls. They prowled through the kitchen. They slunk down the halls. And all was well until the brother mice made the mistake of showing themselves to Mrs. Terwiggle.

"Out! Get out!"

They did for a while. But soon they were back to chatter and chew.

"Why do all of the mice come to my house?" wondered Mrs. Terwiggle. "Maybe my house is just not clean enough."

She swept the floors and shook out the rugs. She scrubbed the cupboards and hid all the food. She bought a garbage can with a very tight lid.

"That should do it," said Mrs. Terwiggle.

Wrong.

Mice aren't dumb. They simply moved out until she finished her housework.

One rainy day Mrs. Terwiggle bought a piano. The mice took a fancy to it. They danced on the keys singing, "Squeak, squeak, squeak," and "Squeaky-dee-dee."

Mrs. Terwiggle was fond of music, but not when it came from a mangle of mice. "Out! Get out!" she screamed. "Enough is enough," and she called her friend, Mrs. Boomniggle.

Mrs. Boomniggle lives on a farm. Behind her house is a very large barn. And in the barn live a clutter of cats. These are no ordinary cats. These are *mousers*—trained to hunt and—well—take care of mice.

"I have just the cat for you," said Mrs. Boomniggle. "I will give you Ralph. He's the son of my best mouser. Ralph will solve your problem."

Wrong.

Ralph loved music, no matter who made it. Ralph had no argument with mice. Ralph liked to eat the kind of food that came from a box or a can. Ralph liked to sleep. A lot.

At first the mice didn't know this, and they scurried outside. But soon they were back, tickling the piano keys with their tiny paws and singing, "Squeaky-dee-dee."

Mrs. Terwiggle was a wreck. She couldn't sleep. She ignored the birds, the flowers, and the children next door. She no longer enjoyed the wide blue sky and sunshine. She came to hate rainy days.

Mrs. Boomniggle gave her some mousetraps and cheese. "Do you want me to take Ralph away? I could lend you Ralph's father for a while."

Cats, traps, mice, and cheese? This was all too much for Mrs. Terwiggle, who never wanted to hurt the mice. She only wanted them gone—outside—to where mice belong.

"No," she said. "This will not do."

Mrs. Terwiggle started to pack. Mrs. Terwiggle was moving away.

Mice aren't dumb. At first they were happy, but then they grew sad.

Mrs. Terwiggle would take away her food and her piano. She would send Ralph home. And no mouse could have a kinder cat to fear than Ralph.

One mouse left, and then another. Two more left, and then their brothers. Next went the aunt mice and uncle mice and cousin mice. When the sister mice left, they waved good-bye to Mrs. Terwiggle.

At first Mrs. Terwiggle was happy, but then she grew sad. "Where will they go? What will they eat? What music will they make?"

Mrs. Terwiggle unpacked her things. She put on her best hat and drove to the grocery store.

From a corner of the flower garden, the mice watched her return. Ralph woke up from a nap as Mrs. Terwiggle carried a large bag into the garden. Out of the bag came sunflower seeds, millet seeds, and thistle seeds.

For the rest of the day, Mrs. Terwiggle stayed busy. She was building a house—a very small house—especially for mice. And when the job was done, she furnished the house with a very small piano. The piano had keys that played real music.

Mrs. Terwiggle was pleased. "A house for the mice and a house for me. Food for the mice and food for me. A piano for the mice and a piano for me."

The mice were extremely pleased.

Birds sang in the trees. Flowers blossomed in the garden. The children next door came out to play. The wide blue sky and the sunshine made everything seem perfect. And it was.

MAIL FROM MANDY

By Cheryl Fusco

T.C. acted brave when Mom and I stopped by to see her on our way out of town.

"My ankle doesn't hurt," T.C. told us. She was sitting on the sofa with her left leg stretched out on a chair. A big purple pillow cushioned her bandaged left ankle.

T.C. said, "My folks bought me these books and a paint set. I won't get bored."

A little later, T.C. watched from a window as our car pulled away from the curb. I wished things had gone as we'd planned. T.C. was supposed to come with us.

Two days before we left, though, T.C. sprained her ankle. She jumped from the top step of a staircase at school. Classes had just ended; T.C. was so excited about summer vacation and this trip that she jumped.

And fell.

Poor T.C.

As we drove away, Mom said, "Mandy, let's buy Theresa Christina a souvenir of our trip."

Our first stop was a hundred miles from home. We ate lunch in a building that had a gift shop inside it.

"Look around," Mom said. "See if you can find something here."

Crammed onto the shelves of the gift shop were all sorts of things. I saw thimbles, key rings, mugs, plates, glasses, and spoons. But I didn't see anything quite right for my friend.

T.C. doesn't sew. She doesn't need to carry keys yet. And I don't think eating utensils would thrill her at all. (Dishwashing is T.C.'s least favorite chore.)

After a while, Mom came over and said, "Find anything? We should get back on the road soon."

I sighed. "Mom," I said, "what T.C. wants is to share this trip with us."

"Well," Mom said, "have you seen anything here that will make Theresa Christina feel like she took the trip, too?"

Mom gave me a few more minutes to look around. I walked through the aisles and thought about what she had said. Fishing, boating, and hiking were all things T.C. liked. How could I share them with her?

With Mom watching, I quickly picked out colored markers, a notepad, envelopes, and several picture postcards. After we paid for these things, I used some of our change to buy postage stamps from a machine.

On the way to the car, Mom said, "I think you're planning something special for Theresa Christina."

I nodded. "I am."

About 50 miles farther on, we crossed into South Dakota and Mom stopped at an information center to get a map. I took a map, too, and I picked up a couple of brochures. At the information center, I mailed a postcard to T.C.

We stopped to rest several more times before we reached Custer State Park, where Mom had rented a cabin. The cabin was great. It was small but right in the woods near Sylvan Lake. After we unpacked, I sat at a wooden table inside the cabin and wrote T.C. a letter. I marked our route on the map and put the map in the envelope. With markers, I drew our cabin. I put my drawing in the envelope, too.

Every day of the trip, I sent something to T.C. I drew her pictures of the rainbow trout we caught at Sylvan Lake (Mom cleaned and cooked them), of the boat we used (foot pedals instead of paddles moved it), and of the trees we saw during our hikes. (A guidebook helped us identify Ponderosa Pine, Paper Birch, White Spruce, and Quaking Aspen. I liked the Paper Birch best. According to the guidebook, early explorers, like Lewis and Clark, wrote on strips of its strong white bark, and Native Americans covered canoes with it.) I sent postcards, too, of the wildlife we saw—pheasants, squirrels, donkeys, and buffalo.

Driving home, I wondered if T.C. had enjoyed the things I'd sent her. Someday she might learn to sew. Should I have bought her the thimble?

We got home on a Friday night. I went over to T.C.'s early Saturday morning.

When she opened the door, T.C. cried, "Mandy, I'm almost sorry to see you!"

I thought she must not have liked the things I sent her.

Maybe T.C. guessed what I was thinking. She pulled me inside and explained, "While you were away, two o'clock sharp was the best part of each day." (She said that's when the postal carrier usually walked up her sidewalk.)

"Now that you're home, I won't get any more mail," T.C. said. "Your letters and drawings were great. They made me feel like I was right there with you."

"Really?" I asked.

"Yes," T.C. said. "Here, I have something for you."

She took a scrapbook from behind the music stand on the piano, and she handed it to me. Construction paper letters were glued to the cover:

MANDY'S SUMMER VACATION
BY
MANDY AND T.C.

"Sit down," T.C. said.

The two of us sat on the couch, and I opened the scrapbook. Taped inside the front cover was the map I had sent. The postcards, my drawings, even my letters—T.C. had taped them all inside the scrapbook.

"Look at this," she said.

She turned a page, and I saw a watercolor painting of a girl standing at the edge of a lake. The girl's hair was red, like mine. She held a fishing pole. A fish dangled from the end of it. The fish was as big as the girl.

"I tried to make my paintings fit your descriptions exactly," T.C. said.

"Well," I said, "the fish may really have been a bit smaller."

Both of us grinned. Together, we looked at every page in the scrapbook. Everything I had sent T.C. was in it. She'd added lots of her own paintings, too.

When we'd finished looking at the scrapbook and talking about it, T.C. handed it to me.

I said, "No, T.C., you keep the scrapbook. I made those letters and drawings for you."

But she said, "No, Mandy. I made those paintings for you."

In the end, we decided to share the scrapbook. Good friends can find ways to share just about anything, I guess.

Except, perhaps, a sprained ankle.

A BOOK
for
MRS. PORTER

By Sally Lee

Tony bounded up the dimly lit stairs and knocked at Mrs. Porter's door. His knock was soon answered.

"Come in, Tony," the woman said warmly.

Tony smiled. He was glad Mrs. Porter didn't mind his after-school visits. He didn't like staying alone in his own apartment downstairs while his parents were at work.

"Can we read more about Tom Sawyer today?" Tony asked eagerly, when he got inside. He loved listening to Mrs. Porter's books. They were much better than the books he could read himself.

"Of course we can," Mrs. Porter said. She and Tony sat down at the table. Soon Tony forgot about the streets and apartment buildings outside. At least for a while he was floating down the Mississippi River on a raft, having exciting adventures with Tom Sawyer and Huckleberry Finn.

"I hope we can read more tomorrow," Tony said when Mrs. Porter closed the book. "*Tom Sawyer* is my favorite book. What's yours?"

Mrs. Porter's eyes grew misty. "My favorite was a book of poetry my husband gave me forty years ago. It was called *Leaves of Grass* and was written by Walt Whitman."

"Do you still have it?" Tony asked.

"No, I lost it several years ago," Mrs. Porter sighed. "My husband always gave me books for my birthday."

Tony knew it made Mrs. Porter sad to think of her husband, who had died the year before.

"When is your birthday?" he asked, trying to change the subject.

"As a matter of fact, it's Saturday. But when you're my age, you don't pay attention to birthdays."

That night Tony lay awake thinking about Mrs. Porter. She was more like a grandmother than a neighbor. She always took care of him when he was sick. She always listened to his problems. She even knit him some gloves for Christmas. Now he wanted to do something special for her. Suddenly an idea popped into his head. *I'll get her that book!* he thought.

Tony jumped out of bed and got the money he had been saving for a skateboard. He spilled the coins out on his bed and counted them. "Three dollars and seventeen cents," he said to himself. "I hope that's enough."

Tony thought about the book all week. On Saturday morning he stuffed his money into his pocket. He ran several blocks to a small bookstore and hurried in.

"Do you have a book of poems about grass or leaves or something like that?" he asked nervously.

The clerk thought for a moment. "Oh, you must mean *Leaves of Grass?*"

"Yes, that's it!" Tony said. He smiled brightly.

The clerk took a shiny new book off the shelf. A shiver of excitement went through Tony.

"That will be fifteen dollars and ninety-five cents," the clerk said.

Tony felt sick. "It can't be that much," he said.

"We have it in paperback for five dollars," the clerk suggested.

"I don't have that much either," Tony choked. He ran out of the bookstore. *It's not fair,* he thought angrily. *How can I give Mrs. Porter a birthday present when everything is so expensive?*

Tony ran down the busy sidewalk. He didn't care where he was going. He just wanted to get away. After a while he stopped and leaned up against a wall to catch his breath. When he looked down the street, a large building caught his eye. Suddenly his face brightened. *The library!* he thought excitedly.

He ran down the street and up the steps between two large stone lions. He had seen the library many times but had never been inside. A mixture of fear and excitement filled him as he pushed his way through the large doors. Inside, the library was quiet and eerie. He felt completely lost.

The man at the desk spoke to Tony. "May I help you?" he asked.

"I'm looking for a book called *Leaves of Grass,*" Tony whispered.

"Let's see if it's in," the librarian said.

Tony followed him to a large room. Bookcases stretched from the floor to the ceiling on every wall.

The librarian knew exactly where to find the book. "Now if you will give me your library card, I will check out the book for you," he said.

Tony froze. "Give you my what?" he whispered.

"Your library card. Don't you have one?"

Tony shook his head. Tears welled up in his eyes as he spilled out his long story. He told about how special the book was to Mrs. Porter and how he had tried to buy it for her but didn't have enough money.

The librarian thought for a moment. "You seem like a very responsible boy," he said. "I am going to give you a library card. Remember, you must bring the book back in two weeks."

Tony was so excited he nearly flew out of the library with the book tucked under his arm. As soon as he got home, he wrapped it in paper and tied it with a ribbon. Then he dashed upstairs to Mrs. Porter's apartment and knocked on the door.

"Happy Birthday," he said when Mrs. Porter answered the door. He pushed the package into her hand.

"A birthday present for me?" Mrs. Porter said in surprise. She slowly unwrapped the package. "Oh Tony!" she gasped. Lovingly she lifted the book from the wrappings. "This is my favorite book. How did you ever remember?"

"It's only from the library," Tony said quickly. "I'll have to take it back in two weeks. I didn't have enough money to buy it for you."

Mrs. Porter put her arms around Tony and gave him a hug. Her face was glowing. "I will never forget this present, Tony. It's the nicest surprise I have ever had."

Life
with the
Shipples

By Susan Cleaver

My first morning at the Shipples' started a lot earlier than I'd planned. Piano music drifted up the stairs at six o'clock. This was no place for a girl who wanted to sleep in. I put on my robe and went downstairs.

The Shipples' daughter Andrea looked up from the piano. "Good morning, Tracy," she said, much too cheerfully. She was even dressed already.

I remembered the first time I'd met Andrea. It was a few years before, when I was nine and she was eight. She showed up at a picnic in a white dress. Somehow she kept it clean the whole day.

I wandered toward the kitchen. The Shipples' house was unbearably neat. It was like living in a wax museum.

My parents had a house picked out for us here in Ormanton. We'd be moving in a few weeks, but soccer started now, and school would be opening in two days. So I had to be here early.

It was hard to believe the Shipples were friends of my parents. They didn't seem to have anything in common.

"Good morning, Tracy," said Mrs. Shipple, when I walked into the kitchen. "Green will be your color while you're here."

I sat down at my green place mat. Mrs. Shipple was right. I was beginning to feel green already . . . right in the middle of my stomach.

Mr. Shipple sat across from me. I tried not to smile, but this was the first time I'd ever seen him without his toupee.

Andrea came out to the table. "Are you going to my piano recital tonight, Tracy?" she asked.

Mrs. Shipple answered for me. "Of course she is."

"We're all looking forward to it," said Mr. Shipple.

After breakfast Andrea took me to her room to see her hamster. His name was Thor. I tried to hold him, but his feet never stopped moving. He was one of those rumpled-looking hamsters with fur the color of coffee ice cream.

"I'm going to practice the piano some more," said Andrea. "Just put him back in his cage when you're done."

When it was time to get ready for soccer, I put Thor away and got dressed.

I had fun at soccer practice, but it was really hot outside. I felt like a wilted daisy when I got back to the house. I dragged myself into the bathroom with my green towel and my green washcloth and took a shower.

After dinner we went to the recital. I sat down and looked at my program. Andrea's songs were last on the schedule.

I was really tired by the time it was Andrea's turn. The first song she played sounded like a lullaby.

The next thing I remembered was a tap on the shoulder from Mrs. Shipple. "Wake up, Tracy," she said. "It's time to go home."

How embarrassing! The people from the row in front of us were staring at me.

Soon after we got home, Andrea called us into her room.

Thor's cage was empty. I had that green feeling in my stomach again.

"I guess I didn't latch the door," I said. "I'm sorry, Andrea."

"Don't worry, girls," said Mr. Shipple. "We'll put the cage on the floor and prop the door open."

"I'm sure he'll come back when he's hungry," said Mrs. Shipple.

In the morning, there were sunflower-seed shells on the living room carpet. But Thor was still hiding.

At breakfast, Mr. Shipple asked, "How was soccer yesterday?"

"It was great," I said. "We're having a practice game today."

"That sounds like fun," said Mrs. Shipple. "May we come and watch? I'd like to learn about soccer."

"Sure," I said.

At the scrimmage, I played fullback. Near the end of the game, I got the ball away from their best player. But my aim was off, and the ball sailed into the goal. I'd scored for the other team.

And as if that weren't embarrassing enough, the Shipples *cheered* for me. They didn't know the first thing about soccer. For one desperate minute, I really missed my parents.

That night when I was getting ready for bed, I heard Mrs. Shipple scream. We all rushed into her room. There we saw Mr. Shipple's toupee moving across the floor. Then the toupee stopped, and Thor ran out from under it.

Mr. Shipple laughed and scooped up the hamster in both hands. "I don't recall your asking to borrow my hairpiece!" he said to Thor.

"How did he get under there?" Andrea asked.

"My toupee must have fallen off the dresser. I guess Thor crawled under it," said Mr. Shipple.

"I'm sorry I caused all this confusion," I said.

"Things needed a little shaking up around here," said Mrs. Shipple.

"That's what we like about your parents," said Mr. Shipple. "They make us laugh. They're always full of surprises."

"We'll miss you when you leave," said Andrea.

"I'll miss you, too," I said. And *that* was a big surprise for me.

Andrea took Thor to her room. I stopped there on my way to bed.

"Andrea, would you teach me to play the piano?" I asked.

"Sure," she said. "I can give you lessons before school in the mornings."

After that, *every* morning at the Shipples' started a lot earlier than I'd planned.

HIKE UP THE MOUNTAIN

By Marie A. Wright

Mr. Martin noticed that Bill Ryan, the newest member of the club, was lagging behind. He called to the other boys to stop. When Bill caught up, Mr. Martin noticed that Bill's thin, freckled face was very pale. He looked unhappy.

"Are we hiking too fast?" Mr. Martin asked. "We don't want anyone to fall behind and get lost. The trail's hard to follow, and the path up the mountain is getting steeper."

As he talked, the boys gathered around. They looked at Bill curiously. They did not know him very well. He was a newcomer, but he was Mike's neighbor and friend.

Bill fastened the pack securely on his back and shuffled his feet. "I—I don't feel good," he said.

Mike stared at him, shocked and a little angry. Imagine starting off on a hike and camp-out if you didn't feel well! For a moment Mike wished Bill Ryan wasn't his friend. He looked around at the five other boys and met their accusing stares.

Mr. Martin said, "It's too bad you're sick, Bill. What's the matter? Is it your stomach?"

Bill shook his head. "No, it's my tooth. I—I have an—an awful toothache."

"Is the pain really bad?" Mr. Martin asked. "Do you want to go on, or do you think you ought to go back home?"

After a moment Bill answered, "I—I guess I should go home, Mr. Martin. I can go back by myself." He started to turn back, but Mr. Martin stopped him.

"You can't go back alone, Bill. I'm responsible for you boys. We couldn't go on, not knowing whether you got back home safely." He looked at his watch. "Let's see, if I go home with Bill, I could be back in an hour and a half or two hours. Everybody should stay here until I get back. You don't know the trail well enough. Unless you promise to stay right here and wait, we'll all have to go back now."

"Mr. Martin," Mike said, "if we stay here two hours we'll miss the excursion boat when we get to the lake. Then we'll have to wait for the afternoon trip."

"And then we won't get to the cabin until tonight," said another boy.

Each of the boys seemed to have something to say. Finally Mr. Martin held up his hand. "Stop it. This might have happened to any of us. I'm sure Bill felt all right when we started. He didn't know his tooth was going to hurt him. Now, are you going to promise to stay here and wait? Mike, you're the oldest. I'll put you in charge."

Mike looked around. He knew the other boys blamed him a little for bringing Bill along. After all, in a way it was his fault. He had brought Bill into the club.

"I've got a good idea, Mr. Martin," he said. "I'll go back with Bill. You go on with the others. If you miss the morning boat it would ruin the camp-out. You know, I'm kind of responsible for Bill."

Mr. Martin thought about it. "Well, I suppose that's sensible, Mike. We'll be sorry to lose you this time, but there'll be other trips. I hope you boys appreciate what Mike is doing."

Mr. Martin looked around at the other boys. They were grinning now that the hike could go on.

Mike and Bill started back along the trail. Mike was annoyed. Bill should never have started out with them. Then he thought about Bill who looked so sad. He had been a good friend during the past few weeks, the best neighbor Mike had ever had. Maybe Bill was really in pain.

When the path widened enough so they could walk together, Bill said miserably, "I know you're mad at me, Mike. I thought Mr. Martin would let me go home alone. I'm sorry. I ruined your day."

Mike shrugged. "Forget it. It's done now." But Bill looked so unhappy that Mike felt ashamed of himself. "Let's talk about something else," he said.

"Oh, sure—uh—I suppose all the kids will go swimming. Do you know how to swim?"

Mike gave him a disgusted look. Did Bill think that was a different subject? He said grumpily, "No, I don't swim very well. There isn't any place to swim around here. I wish we had a pool. Then I could get some practice."

"There's a pool at Grove City," answered Bill.

"I know, but Grove City's too far away. Why, do you ever go there to swim?"

"No, I don't. But I've thought about it. They give lessons—twice a week."

Mike dropped the subject. He didn't feel much like talking anyway.

Mike left Bill at his house, after explaining to Bill's mother about the trip. She looked upset but thanked him. He went home where his mother greeted him with surprise and listened to his story. When he finished, she told him they would make it up to him some way. "Maybe a picnic in the park tomorrow," she said.

Mike answered, "It's still not the same as the camp-out."

Mike was in his room after supper when his father called him. "Come on down, Mike. Bill's mother and father are here. They want to see you."

Mike wished they had stayed home, but he went downstairs. Mr. and Mrs. Ryan thanked him and he said, "That's okay." Then he added, "I hope Bill is better. I know a toothache can be really painful."

"That's what we wanted to see you about, Mike," said Mr. Ryan. "You see, Bill didn't really have a toothache."

Mike stared. "He didn't! Then what—?"

"Well, Bill was afraid of the boat on the water. He wanted very much to go with you, but as he got nearer and nearer the lake, he got more and more frightened."

39

Bill's mother explained, "Last year Bill and his father nearly drowned when we were on the coast. Their boat upset when they were fishing in the sound. It took a long time to revive Bill. We thought he wouldn't pull through. Since then, the water terrifies him. We think he'll be all right if he learns to swim. And he wants to learn."

Mike listened with mixed feelings. Anger that he had been cheated—sympathy for Bill—scorn for his cowardice—all whirled together in his mind. Why did they have to tell him? He turned to his father with an appealing look.

His father smiled and put his arm around Mike's shoulder. "Bill's mother thought you and Bill might like to go to the Grove City pool for swimming classes," he said. "Bill won't go alone. But he said he'd go if you would go with him. Would you like to?"

Mike swallowed hard. Like it? He'd love it. A chance to swim twice a week and take lessons. He nodded.

Mr. Ryan stood up. "Well, that's that, then. It's good of you to help. He thinks a lot of you, Mike."

Mrs. Ryan said, "We'll go to Grove City on Monday afternoon after school. Will that be all right?"

A smile spread across Mike's face. "It will be great! Tell Bill I'll be waiting for him on Monday."

The Girl Who Sang to Plants

By Carolyn Bowman

Mrs. Dillon was announcing a class project, one that didn't interest Mindy at all.

"For three weeks," Mrs. Dillon was saying, "you'll be growing plants. I'll expect you to keep an accurate record of how often you water them, how many hours of sun they receive, what—if any—types of plant food you use. . . ."

Mindy tried to pay attention, but her mind was wandering. Soon the bell would ring. Soon she'd be on the pitchers' mound, hurling bullets to the team from Redville. Her team, the Wilmont Raiders, was undefeated. Mindy planned to do her share to keep it that way.

"You'll each work with a partner on this project," Mrs. Dillon said.

That snapped Mindy out of her daydream. She looked over at her best friend, Chelsey, as their teacher continued.

"This is homework, so you and your partner can decide where to keep your plant. You'll agree on a schedule and work as a team. May the best plant win."

"What's the prize?" asked Chelsey.

This pleased Mindy. Chelsey probably knew as little about plants as she did, but Chelsey played first base for their team. They both loved to compete, and win.

Mrs. Dillon said, "The winners will be given enough seeds to grow the best vegetable garden in town this summer."

Mindy didn't really care about the prize. Winning was what mattered.

Chelsey's smile showed that she agreed.

With attendance book in hand, Mrs. Dillon began to announce partners.

She was picking them herself! Mindy crossed her fingers, hoping that she and Chelsey would be paired up. She tried to cross her toes, but her sneakers wouldn't allow it. She listened to their teacher say, "Chelsey and Harriet . . . Mindy and Anne."

Anne? Mindy couldn't believe it! Anne hated softball. As far as Mindy knew, Anne hated *all* sports. She liked to dance, an activity Mindy avoided.

Doing some quick calculating, Mindy realized she'd be spending a lot of time with Anne. She and Chelsey could have easily taken care of a plant after practice and games. Getting together with Anne *would* be homework; the worst kind.

That afternoon, the Wilmont Raiders lost their game. Mindy gave up five runs—two of them, homers. She was in no mood to see Anne. But Anne was waiting on Mindy's porch.

"This is a night-blooming cereus," Anne said. "If you like, we can use it for our project."

The plant was the strangest Mindy had ever seen. Stuck in a jug of water, it was tall with twisted branches. Its leaves were long—almost like fingers—and from each leaf grew other leaves. Mindy touched one. It was as smooth and moist as butter.

"Weird," she said.

"These are roots." Anne pointed to the brown hairy bits springing out along the branches.

Mindy wondered at the ball of wormy-looking roots already choking the bottom of the jug.

Anne seemed to read her thoughts. "We can plant it in a pot, then it will grow better. I always start my seedlings in water."

"Seedlings?" Mindy said. "You seem to know a lot about plants."

"Some say."

Mindy couldn't take her eyes off the night-blooming cereus. It reminded her of a plant that had once starred in a movie, a plant that—*ate people.* "Does this plant *do* anything?" she asked.

"It's lousy at softball," Anne said. "But it dances in a breeze."

With a laugh, Mindy said, "Okay, let's get this over with. Your house or mine?"

They settled on Anne's, because her family had a greenhouse.

In the days that followed, Mindy set aside more and more time to work with Anne on their plant project. Chelsey and Harriet were busy with a geranium. "That is *so* ordinary," Mindy told Anne, as they cared for their night-blooming cereus.

Into a large pot—that they painted in swirling designs—went their plant. Daily notes stated that (1) the cereus required a drink every seven days; because it was a cactus it was best to let it dry out between waterings, (2) it seemed to prefer indirect sun (3) that one serving of plant food was enough to last for six months, and (4) that it responded to singing—

Anne's idea. In fact, Anne sang to *all* her plants. And when she wasn't there to sing, she put music on her tape recorder—Mozart—the cereus loved Mozart! *It was all so weird,* Mindy thought, *but fabulous.*

Other weird things were happening. Anne attended softball games and cheered Mindy on to victory. Mindy attended dance classes and cheered Anne onto her toes.

Then, the three-week project came to an end. The two girls took the cereus to class *and* won the prize. That afternoon, they carried their seed packets and the plant to Anne's house.

"It's been fun," Mindy said, and she meant it. A sad feeling welled up inside of her. She was worried that their friendship might end.

"Don't look so *ce-re-us!*" Anne said. "We're going to have lots more fun growing our garden."

"We are?"

"You can count on it." Anne arranged the seed packets to show the vegetables they would grow.

"Carrots, cucumbers, onions, tomatoes . . . this is so cool!"

"There's something I haven't told you about the cereus," Anne said.

Visions of man-eating plants filled Mindy's head. Now the truth was coming out.

"It really *does* bloom. It makes a flower, but I've been told that happens only once a year—in August—at midnight."

"What?" The idea was too wild for Mindy to believe. "You're teasing."

"You'll see. I'll call you when it's happening. Then, you'll have to hurry over—"

"At midnight. *Crazy,*" Mindy said. She would be there. She wouldn't miss it for the world.

VALENTINES AND ORANGE PEELS

By Nancy Garber

Matt took the subway to school every day. He counted the steps down to the station and up again. He always tried to get the eleventh seat on his subway car, just because he liked the number eleven. Sometimes the fat man got on before Matt and got seat eleven, and then Matt had to take whatever seat he could get.

Matt liked anything to do with numbers. He counted the cracks in the sidewalk from the subway station to the newsstand on the corner, and sometimes he bumped into people because his head was down.

"Hey, Matt," his friend Agnes called out. "You'd better watch where you're going." Agnes ran the newsstand, and she was the most interesting-looking woman he'd ever seen. She had wiry gray hair that looked just like steel wool where it escaped from the bun in the back. She wore thick tan stockings and old slippers on her feet, and a man's sweater covered her almost to the knees, hot days or cold.

And her dog, Kate, loved orange peels. Every morning on the way to the station Matt brought Kate an orange peel to chomp on, and she wagged her stubby tail and licked him for it. Kate had four tufts of black hair (Matt counted them, of course) and the rest of her was a wiry gray, like Agnes's hair. In cold weather Kate sat on Agnes's feet in the old slippers; that way they both kept warm.

There was a lot of black slushy snow piled up in front of the newsstand one day in February. "A hard winter," Agnes said. "A hard winter." Then she turned to the men and women hurrying by, their collars clutched against the cold. "*Examiner!* Get the latest *Examiner!*" she called in her reedy voice.

Matt was sort of in a hurry because this was Valentine's Day, and he could hardly wait to get to school to work on the card for his mom. But when he saw how wet Agnes's slippers were and how soggy poor Kate's tail was, he grabbed the old broom inside the stand and started to sweep the slush away.

"You don't have time for that, Matt," Agnes said. "I'll do it later. You'll be late for school."

"It will just take a minute," Matt said. "I'll hurry." The slush was dark and heavy, but he pushed at it with the broom until it sloshed into the street, and then he ran for his train.

On the way home from school that day, Matt didn't count the steps to the station. He didn't look for seat eleven. He almost walked right by Agnes and Kate without seeing them.

"Hey, Matt," Agnes called. "Why the long face? Your girl turn you down?"

"I don't have a girlfriend,'" Matt mumbled.

She put her huge hand under his chin. "Well then, what is it? Kate and I don't like to see sadness on the face of our favorite friend."

Matt said, "I lost the valentine I made for Mom. I lost it somewhere on the playground. I don't know where I lost it."

"Of course you don't. If you did, you could find it."

"Agnes, I made this nice valentine—you should've seen it. Red shiny paper and a lace heart. All the kids said it was the best one. Now it's gone."

"Don't worry, chum," Agnes said. She reached under the counter. "The fat man from your train gave me this today. His secretary gave it to him, but he's on a diet. You take it to your mom." She held out a tiny, red heart-shaped box of chocolates with To My Valentine on the top.

The red box flashed in the street light. How his mom would love the chocolates. But—"It's beautiful," he said, "but it's yours."

"Oh no," Agnes said. "I never eat chocolate. And you know it's not good for dogs. So Kate can't eat it, either." She laughed.

"Oh, Agnes," he said, "do you really mean it?"

"Why not? I can't think of anyone I'd rather give it to than you. You never forget Kate's orange peel, and we've been dry all day because you took the time to sweep the snow for us."

Matt took the box. "My mom will love it, Agnes," he said. "Thank you. And thank you, Kate."

Kate wagged her tail and licked his ankle.

Matt's mom liked the valentine present. After the chocolates were all eaten, Matt kept the little red box by his place at the breakfast table. Every day he put a piece of orange peel in it to take to Kate. He still counted all the steps. And he *always* let the fat man have the eleventh subway seat.

MR. TRINIBY'S SECRET

By Julia F. Lieser

The children on Vinewood Street were curious. Mr. Triniby was building something in the oak tree in his back yard, and they didn't know what it was.

"I think he is building a treehouse," said Martin, as they walked down the street to the school bus stop at the corner.

"A treehouse!" said Sue Ellen. "What would Mr. Triniby want with a treehouse?"

"He could sit in it and read his paper," said Eric.

Dorothy looked doubtful. "Mr. Triniby likes to

read his paper on the porch with Mrs. Triniby. They like to sit together in their rockers. My mom said so," she added for emphasis.

"He's probably building a place to store his lawn furniture and garden tools during the winter," said Martin. "He has a very small garage."

"Why would he want to climb up a ladder to do that?" asked Sue Ellen. "He'd build a storage shed on the ground."

"Hey! We'd better hurry," said Dorothy. "Here comes the bus."

Coming back from the bus stop that afternoon, the children could hear Mr. Triniby hammering in his oak tree. As they approached his house, they could see through the new green leaves that the large platform now had two sides. Mr. Triniby was nailing the frame in place around a small window.

"Oh, look!" said Martin. "I told you he was building a treehouse. He's probably got grandchildren who are coming to visit, and it will be theirs."

"Lucky kids," said Eric.

Dorothy kicked a little stone along the sidewalk with her toe. "My mom said the Trinibys do not have any grandchildren. They had one little boy of their own, who died a long time ago. It's very sad."

Sue Ellen thought a minute. "Why don't we just go and ask Mr. Triniby?"

"At least we'd know," said Eric. "Then we could stop wondering."

"Okay," said Martin, taking charge. "I'll do the asking."

The four children filed past Mrs. Triniby's bed of roses by the back porch and lined up under the oak tree. Mr. Triniby smiled down.

"Hi, gang," he said.

"Hello," they chorused. They didn't know Mr. Triniby very well. He had moved to town only a few months before.

Martin cleared his throat and stuck one hand in his back pocket. "Uh-mm, Mr. Triniby, we've been wondering what you're building up in that oak tree of yours."

Mr. Triniby climbed down the stepladder and laid his hammer on the top step. His face was serious, but his eyes were merry.

"I'd like to tell you," he said, smiling, "but it's a secret. A big secret. I gave my word that I wouldn't tell."

"Oh," said Sue Ellen, disappointed. "Will you be allowed to tell sometime?"

"Well, now let's see," said Mr. Triniby. "This is Tuesday and . . . why don't you all come here Saturday afternoon. Around one o'clock will be good," said Mr. Triniby.

"All right," said Martin slowly. "Is that when you'll be allowed to tell?"

"I'll arrange it," Mr. Triniby said, and winked. "See you Saturday."

On Wednesday afternoon the treehouse had four sides and a doorway. Thursday afternoon it had a roof, and on Friday afternoon it had a fresh coat of green paint that matched the color of the new green leaves. The children could not wait to find out about Mr. Triniby's secret.

At one o'clock on Saturday, the four children hurried past Mrs. Triniby's roses and saw Mrs. Triniby on the back porch. She was setting the picnic table with paper plates and cups. In the middle of the table was a cake covered with candles.

"Is Mr. Triniby here?" asked Martin. "He told us to come at one o'clock."

"Yes, he's here," answered Mrs. Triniby. "He'll be right out."

"Whose birthday is it?" asked Sue Ellen.

"Mr. Triniby's. Didn't he tell you?" The children all shook their heads.

"Oh, that Norton!" said Mrs. Triniby, and laughed.

Just then the screen door opened, and the children all shouted "Happy Birthday!"

Mr. Triniby leaned back against the house, the sudden outburst having taken him by surprise.

"Thank you," he said finally. "You really did startle me."

"Are you going to tell us about the treehouse now?" asked Martin.

"Yes, he is," said Mrs. Triniby, "but first let's have some birthday cake," she said, lighting the many, many candles.

"You mean the party's for us?" asked Eric.

"You bet! You all like chocolate cake, don't you?" asked Mr. Triniby.

When the cake and ice cream were eaten up and the cups of punch finished, Mr. Triniby leaned back. The children waited expectantly. Finally he began to talk.

"My daddy used to say we should be grateful for each birthday we are privileged to reach, and for that reason we should *give* gifts to others on our birthdays. So, I built the treehouse to give to you on my birthday."

The four children all stared at him, speechless.

"You mean it's ours?" said Eric. "Just like that?"

"On two conditions," continued Mr. Triniby. "First, it will be your job to keep the leaves raked up in the fall."

"Oh, that's not hard. That's fun," said Sue Ellen.

"And second, —well, you see, when I was a boy I always wanted a treehouse. I never had one. So, will you let me come up and sit in yours once in a while?"

"Oh, yes," they chorused. "Every day if you like. Thank you. Thank you, Mr. Triniby," and they all hugged him.

Then Dorothy stepped back and looked at Mr. Triniby. "Who made you promise not to tell, when it was your secret?"

Mr. Triniby threw back his head and laughed. "My dear wife. She said I could never keep a secret, but I fooled her this time." And he winked at Mrs. Triniby.

All summer the children on Vinewood Street enjoyed the treehouse. Mrs. Triniby brought them warm cookies and cold fruit juices on hot afternoons. They were no longer curious about the Tranibys. They were sure they were the best friends any kids ever had.

They Need Boys in Ballet

By Linda Roberts

"I'm never going back!" said Allen. "I hate ballet! I wish I'd never signed up for it."

Allen and his mother were walking out to their car. "Were the girls giggling again?" asked his mother.

"Yeah. They always laugh at me."

Allen had known on the first day that he had made a mistake when he decided to take ballet. His mother had told him what the secretary said. He'd be the only boy. She asked if he'd mind that.

"No, why should I?" said Allen. He had seen men ballet dancers on TV, and it was wonderful the way they could leap and spin. He had read library books about ballet. The books said that there were usually more girls than boys in a class, but that meant boys were important. They needed boys in ballet.

But Allen had started a few weeks after the classes began. As he walked in, the other students were standing at the barre in front of the big mirrors. All of them were girls. They looked at him in his tights, then at each other. They covered their mouths and giggled.

Allen's face felt hot. He walked to a place at the end of the line and looked at the floor.

"Welcome, Allen," said Ms. Maria, the teacher. "We're very glad to have you." She started the music, and they did warm-up exercises. Then she said, "Time to practice pliés. Turn out, everyone. Backs straight! Plié!"

Slowly, everyone pliéd, bending their knees with one hand on the barre. Stiffly, Allen did the same. It was hard to do without bending forward. Ms. Maria helped him.

When class was over, Allen left right away.

Soon the kids at school heard that Allen was taking ballet.

"Ballet!" said Jason, when they went out for recess. "That's sick. Ballet's for girls. Why would you take ballet? I'm taking karate."

"Shut up," said Allen.

"You shut up," said Jason, and started scooping up snow.

"Boys," said Mrs. Montgomery, "no talking like that, and no throwing snowballs."

Jason spent recess pretending to do ballet. He twirled around in the snow with silly expressions on his face while the other kids laughed. Allen sat by himself on top of the monkey bars.

When he went home, he told his mother what he had decided. "I'm not going back," he said. "I hate being the only boy. From now on, I'm sticking with baseball."

"Allen, I'm sorry it's like this," said his mother. "Is it dancing you don't like, or is it the other kids that make it hard?"

"Well, I guess I do like dancing," he said slowly. "But I wish there was one other boy there. Just one."

"I can understand that. But if you really like to dance, it's a shame to stop because of the other kids. Look, at least finish this course. Then if you don't want to sign up again, you don't have to."

His next lesson was that afternoon. Only three more to go. He pulled on his tights and T-shirt, putting his jeans and jacket over them, and rode all the way in the car without saying a word.

When he got there, he stood at the barre next to Laura and Jenny. At least they didn't laugh at him. He liked to talk to them sometimes.

Then a new girl came in with her mother. They went up to Ms. Maria. He heard Ms. Maria say, "Hello, Kristal. We're so glad to have you."

Kristal didn't say anything. She stood close to her mother.

Allen heard Kristal's mother say softly, "Honey, you'll do fine." She kissed her and left.

Kristal looked scared. "There's a place, Kristal," said Ms. Maria, pointing toward the end of the line next to Allen. Kristal slowly walked toward him with her head down. Allen felt sorry for her.

Ms. Maria helped Kristal with her pliés. "Backs straight," said Ms. Maria, but Kristal kept bending forward. Her face was red. Allen heard a giggle from one of the girls. He wanted to help Kristal, but how? When it was time to take partners for a new step they were learning, Kristal hung her head and looked at the floor.

Then Allen knew what to do. "Hey, Kristal," he said, "you want to be my partner?"

Kristal looked up for the first time. "Okay," she whispered.

Ms. Maria stood in front and led the class. Kristal tried to follow the movements.

"No, the other foot," whispered Allen. "Yeah, like that." Kristal watched Allen. She stepped ahead, behind, and then turned, the way he did. In a few minutes, they could do the step.

"That's good," said Allen. "Hey, Laura, look at us."

Laura and Jenny smiled at Kristal. Kristal shyly smiled back.

On their way home that day, Allen said, "Mom, I've been thinking. Maybe I will keep taking ballet. For a while, anyway."

"You will? That's great! What brought this on?"

"Well, I think it's fun. And anyway, they need boys in ballet."

FRIEND IN SIGHT

By Janet Rice Finney

Lorraine looked in the mirror. Slowly turning her head from side to side, she inspected her new glasses.

"Fish eyes, that's what I've got. Fish eyes."

"You'll get used to them in no time," said the eye doctor. He leaned forward almost into her face to adjust the glasses. "There. Now doesn't that feel better?" he asked brightly.

"No." Lorraine shrugged. "I won't wear them home," she said defiantly.

She put the glasses in their bright blue case. She and her mother walked out to the car.

"May I listen to the radio?" asked Lorraine.

"Sure," said her mother. Lorraine started twirling the dial. "That's the knob to the heater," her mother said quietly.

"I know that!" Lorraine barked. "I can see. I'm just cold." She moved her hand to the radio dial.

That evening after dinner Lorraine climbed into bed, arranging her stuffed animals in a row beside her. "I'm going to read you a story," she announced. Opening her book, she propped it in front of the big white bear about two feet away. The words were just a smudge across the page, and she had to move the book until it was a few inches in front of her nose.

In the morning Lorraine hid her new glasses under the peony bush in front of the house. With a big sigh she stepped to the curb and waited for the school bus. The big orange-and-black mass coming down the road stopped in front of Lorraine. After climbing up the steps, she sat quickly in the first empty seat.

"Look what you did!" yelled a red-haired kid, hovering over her. Lorraine didn't want to look. "You ruined my volcano! Mrs. Gordon will kill me!" yelled the kid, even louder.

"I didn't see it," said Lorraine meekly. She stood up, mud and paint dripping down her legs.

"Didn't see it? What are you, blind?"

Lorraine ran to the back of the bus. She stared out the window. Everything was a mixture of colors streaking past her. It must be because of the tears, she thought.

"Attention, class," called Mrs. Gordon. "Put all your books away. Today we're going to study the continents. Look at the map on the board, and write the names of the continents on the map I'm going to pass out to you."

"I'm in trouble," said Lorraine to herself. The map on the board looked like white clouds on a blue-green sky—with no letters.

Lorraine looked around the classroom. She saw the globe on the windowsill next to her. Quietly she got up and twirled it around close to her eyes until she could read the names of the continents.

"Lorraine's cheating!" shouted a voice from the back of the room. Lorraine could feel the stares of the class. Humiliated, she sat down.

After school, Lorraine picked up her glasses from beneath the peony bush and shoved them into her pocket. Then she went for a walk in the park.

She saw a girl sitting on a wooden bench with a black suitcase beside her.

Maybe she's moving to a new town. *Maybe that's what I should do,* thought Lorraine. She sat down on the end of the bench.

"Hello," said the girl, smiling. "Do you visit the park often?"

"Sometimes," answered Lorraine.

"I like the geese that feed at the pond best. They sound so excited, honking all the time."

"Uh-huh," answered Lorraine.

The suitcase suddenly came alive and stood up.

"Yikes!" yelled Lorraine. "Is that your dog?"

"It's all right, Randy," said the girl, patting the dog's head. "He's friendly. Don't worry."

Lorraine looked more closely at the big dog sitting next to her. She stood up.

"Are you leaving?" asked the girl.

"I'm just going for a walk."

"Do you mind if I walk with you?" The girl stood up. Randy moved closer to her. "Let's go down to the pond. I'd like to listen to the geese," she said.

They sat down on the grass. Lorraine saw the water as blurred sparkles in the sunlight. "That bullfrog sure makes a lot of noise," the girl said with a laugh. "Are the turtles sunning themselves on the log today?"

Lorraine turned and stared. "You mean that you can't see them either?"

"I'm blind," the girl said softly. "Didn't you know? Are you blind, too?"

"Oh, no," Lorraine answered.

"Then why can't you tell if the turtles are there?"

"I don't have my glasses on," said Lorraine.

"Oh. Would you put them on," said the girl, "and tell me about the turtles?"

Lorraine reached in her pocket and pulled out the glasses. They felt heavy on her nose. Suddenly Lorraine's world was clear.

"Across the pond, sitting on a dead tree log," she said, "there are one, two, three . . . four turtles. They're lined up like raisins on peanut butter. And one just fell into the water."

The girl laughed and sat up straighter.

Lorraine looked at her new friend. She was a few years older than Lorraine. Her bright blue eyes reflected the light from the pond. She didn't look blind.

"Tell me more!" the girl said.

"There's a heron on the shore across the pond."

"Is he marching like a soldier?"

"Yes," said Lorraine. "But his knees are wobbly. Oh, now he's flying. He's more graceful in the air than he was on the ground."

The girl stood up. "My name is Sarah. I come here every day. Will you be here tomorrow?"

"Sure. I'll be here."

Sarah started to walk away. Then she stopped and said, "I do wish I could put on glasses and see the world the way you do."

Lorraine watched thoughtfully as Sarah walked away. She was tall and pretty with hair the color of chestnuts. She held tightly to the handle of Randy's special harness.

Lorraine walked slowly home. She could count the ants on the sidewalk. She could count the leaves on the trees. At the far end of the road her mother waved, a small dot in the distance. Lorraine ran to meet her.

One of My Best Friends

By Barbara M. Coe

One of my best friends came over today. We had a really good time, with no fighting.

Even when I jumped off the seesaw, she didn't get mad. When I squirted her with the hose, she just grabbed it and squirted me back. We both said that hose water tastes different. It just tastes like hose water and nothing else. And you know that noise it makes in your mouth? I can't spell it, and neither can she.

She had good ideas. We made a blanket tent in the yard, and it was all blue inside. It looked nice. We ate our lunch in the tent. My sandwich looked blue. That wasn't nice, so I went outside to eat on the grass. My friend stayed in the tent. She told me that was okay, because we could say we were having an inside-out lunch.

And when I took the biggest cookie, she didn't care, even though she had brought them. My friend is like that. And she remembered—no nuts.

We had a plan. We were going to sleep in our tent at night. Then I thought of all the blue inside that might turn black at night. My friend didn't like to think about it, either. Then she said we could just take a nap in our tent. But I said it would take too much time to take a nap. She said I was right, and so we had to make another plan.

We went for a walk down by the seashore. She took off her sneakers first. I wasn't really afraid of the crab we saw, and she knew it. It was a really BIG crab.

When it was low tide, my friend didn't mind the fishy smell. She said it was a good smell. I told her that lots of good things, like baby crabs and baby lobsters, live in the muddy low-tide bottom.

My friend talked softly when we saw the egret. Egrets walk funny, and my friend did it perfectly.

She poked her head forward on her neck, then she picked her feet up high, just like the egret. My friend looked so funny I laughed out loud and scared the bird. But that was all right—my friend laughed, too.

We found lots of shells. I found a yellow one and a black one with white and purple. I carried all my shells home in my pocket, and none of them broke. That was lucky because when we got home, my friend and I made shell-people with glue. She showed me how. We made an egret and put spaghetti legs on it. I told my friend it looked just like her. She laughed.

The best part was when Mom gave us a treat. My friend took the chocolate syrup and drizzled it, real slowly, on her ice cream and wrote her name. I did, too, but my name didn't fit, and I got chocolate on the tablecloth. My friend covered the spot with her napkin so my elbow wouldn't get all sticky. We ate the ice cream, and when it was gone, my friend did something. Boy, was I surprised!

She picked up her ice cream plate and licked it clean! I yelled at her, "Grandma! Don't let Mom see you do that!" Grandma giggled and put down her plate.

Know why Grandma is one of my best friends? She likes me all the time. She doesn't laugh at me, even when I do things that are kind of silly. The thing I like most about Grandma is this—she is so much fun, and boy, can she surprise me!

New Girl

By Marjory A. Grieser

"Ginnie!" Miss Hewlett's voice startled Virginia out of her daydream. She was watching the sparrows flicker in and out of the trees bordering the playground. "Ginnie, I'd like you to meet the other girls."

Ginnie allowed her fifth-grade teacher to guide her to the baseball diamond. She'd already met some of the girls in her new school and hadn't yet decided whether she liked them. Sally, small and pretty, was looking Ginnie over in a way that struck her as unfriendly. Ginnie was a head taller than the others and felt awkward alongside them.

She blushed under Sally's open stare and hid her face as she bent to pick up the bat. She swung it once or twice with the grace of a natural athlete and nodded to the pitcher. When the ball came zinging toward her, she uncoiled and, with a crack of wood against leather, sent the ball flying over the fence.

Ginnie stumbled over home plate and returned to her place in line, breathless with success and exertion.

"Why don't you try out for the boys' team?" Sally tossed her blond curls smartly over her shoulder and giggled. The fun of making the first home run evaporated. Ginnie sat down and blinked back tears of anger and loneliness. She fixed her attention again on the sparrows and hoped the others would think she didn't care. That was when the idea suddenly came to her.

She mentioned her idea casually to her father when he came home from work.

"A bird feeder," he said, nodding thoughtfully. "That's a good idea."

"One I can build myself," Ginnie added. "And I'd like to get some books, too, books with pictures of birds in them."

She heard him mention it to her mother later. "It will give her something to do until she makes friends."

Not likely, Ginnie thought.

"Give her time," her mother replied. "She's never had to move before."

The feeder was simple to build. Ginnie had been handling tools since she was old enough to pick them up. Two evenings and it was finished. She coated it with varnish to protect it from the weather. While the varnish dried, she pored over her book, learning the names of the birds she saw daily in the back yard and in the ravine beyond.

It wasn't long before the feeder was a busy flutter of wings. Ginnie found herself getting up a little earlier in the morning to watch her bird friends as they sang and fought for the best place at the feeder. The song sparrow, his black diamond bright against the streaked white of his breast, woke her with a liquid trill of gratitude for his breakfast. In the evenings a scarlet cardinal called his dusky mate to supper as Ginnie watched them from a distance through her field glasses. A pair of tiny, fearless pine siskins, wings tipped with yellow-green, paused only a second in their busy feeding as Ginnie, book in hand, came near them for a closer look.

She loved them all as she got to know them better. Somehow she felt closer to them than she did to her human companions at school. Ginnie thought of how, after the first three days, no one joined her for lunch. Sally always seemed to be the center of the lunch group. They giggled a lot, and more than once Ginnie felt sure that Sally's laughing comments were about her.

At dinner one evening she pushed her plate away angrily. Her mother raised her eyebrows slightly.

"Miss Hewlett," Ginnie explained grimly. "She wants all of us to stand up and tell the class about our hobbies."

"That's a nice idea." Her mother pushed the plate in front of her.

"I don't have any hobbies!" She ignored the plate and reached for her glass of milk.

"What about your birds?"

Ginnie glared at her mother scornfully. "Nobody's interested in birds."

But she knew she'd have to tell the class about them. What else could she talk about? She dragged herself to bed later, without even checking the feeder.

A lilting warble woke her in the morning. The notes were different from any she'd heard before.

She rubbed the sleep from her eyes and reached for the book and field glasses.

"A white-crowned sparrow—so rare in city yards!" She rushed to the kitchen and shoved the field glasses into her mother's hands. "Look at him. He looks like other sparrows, but he has a black band around his head and the top of his head is white."

But by the time she was ready for school, she remembered that she had to give her talk.

Ginnie was numb when she stood in front of the class. She dropped her book clumsily and heard Sally snickering. Then she took a deep breath and started to talk.

It wasn't as hard as she'd expected. She opened the book to show pictures of the different birds and noticed her classmates moving closer to see them. Sally started to make some sneering remarks, but a boy leaned across the aisle, tapped her on the arm, and shook his head.

Sally looked sullen and alone. *Serves her right,* Ginnie thought. Then she realized that Sally was lonely, too, just as she had been. Sally wanted attention just as she did.

But right now, Ginnie wasn't lonely at all.

One boy raised his hand a little hesitantly. "I liked Ginnie's talk best of all."

Ginnie felt a warm flush of gratitude on her cheeks.

"How do the rest of you feel? How many liked Ginnie's talk best?" Miss Hewlett was smiling.

Suddenly the room was full of hands waving in the air. Even Sally had her hand halfway up, as if she were scared someone might see her.

Then an idea occurred to Ginnie. "I can bring my plans and books to school and show the class how to build a feeder." She wondered why she hadn't thought of it sooner. It would be fun to share with the others. Besides, she could see now that they'd just been waiting for her to show them who she really was!

Randy's Gift for Clem

By Ruth Sexton Sargent

Randy was thinking hard. What could he give to Clem? He didn't have enough money to buy a gift. He wasn't clever at making things. He didn't own anything fine enough to give him. What could he do? He frowned as he sat under a big tree by the brook. Resting his hand on his clenched fist, Randy puzzled over his question.

Clem had been the school custodian for nearly twenty years, and now he was retiring. All that time he had swept the floors, dusted the desks, and cleaned the windows until they sparkled. In the fall he raked the leaves from the grounds, fixed the swings, and kept the sandbox filled for the kindergarteners. On winter mornings he shoveled the snow from the long sidewalk and sprinkled sand on the icy spots. He painted hopscotch games in white paint on the playground and watered flowers in the window boxes in the spring. He counted out the pieces of chalk and erasers for each room, along with the paste pots, scissors, and paints that he kept in a big supply closet. He also had a "lost-and-found" box where you were sure to find your missing mitten or rubber boot. He arranged all the chairs in straight rows in the gym for the programs, and afterward he polished the floor shiny bright again.

Yet, in spite of all his duties, Clem always found time to smile and say hello to everyone. If you lost your milk money in the hallway, Clem could spot it in the corner. If you forgot your mittens on a snowy day, he would stop and rub your hands in his for a few moments till they felt tingling warm. He even had extra buttons he would sew on your coat, if you lost one on the way to school. And no zipper could baffle him! He could always get it unstuck and working smoothly again.

Yes, everyone would miss Clem, thought Randy. And he tried to imagine how many children had known and loved Clem in all those twenty years. Now that Clem was retiring, everyone had brought a nickel to put toward a big gift for him. Some of the kids had even given up buying cookies at noon in order to give a little more. They felt that if they gave their cookie money, it would really be their gift to Clem, not just money their parents had given to them. The teachers had a special present for him, and Beverly's mother was baking one of her fancy cakes for Clem. Randy pictured the assembly program they were going to have on the following day to surprise Clem. The students in each grade had written poems and songs telling how much they would miss him.

But Randy wanted to give Clem a present all his own, so Clem would know how much he meant to him. Clem wanted to go fishing when he retired, Randy remembered. But fishing rods cost a lot. That was what the students had voted to get. When all the nickels had been brought in and counted, there had been enough to buy a very fine fishing rod.

Just then a little noise from the brook caught Randy's attention. He looked toward the water in time to see several small trout splashing along.

There were always fish here to catch, and Randy spent many hours in his secret spot. No one else ever came here, and he had never told anyone about the place. It was quiet and peaceful.

Randy stood up quickly. That was it! That was the answer. He would give Clem the directions for finding his private fishing grounds. He'd draw a little map with exact directions for him to follow. He'd dig a bucket of worms for bait, and he'd even give him his lucky fishing hat with the two fancy flies pinned on it. He never used them, but they looked quite impressive and made him feel as though he knew quite a lot about the sport.

"Yippee!" he shouted, turning a somersault in the grass. He had a gift for Clem after all, one that would last for all his years of retirement.

Make Room for Me!

By Lillian Nordlicht

Fernando stood in the doorway of the rooftop, watching the neighborhood kids flying kites.

"Go away!" they said.

"I only wanted to watch," said Fernando. But he went down the stairs to the street.

He watched some boys playing baseball. He chopped one hand into the other to show he could catch. But no one asked him to join.

He watched other kids playing stickball. He wound up once, twice, three times, and pretended to throw a ball. But no one even looked his way.

There was nothing for Fernando to do but sit down in the doorway of the apartment house he lived in.

"Why did we have to move to this dumb block?" he muttered. He thought of all the friends he had left behind on 110th Street. He missed them a lot.

Suddenly he heard a great roar and rumble. From where he sat, Fernando could see a giant parade of machines coming nearer and nearer. When they came to the empty lot across the street, the dump trucks, cranes, and shovels turned slowly and entered.

Fernando jumped up and ran across the street. Now at last he had something to do. He could watch the steam shovels dig and dump.

But the lot had a high wooden fence around it. Although he could hear the big machines growling with power behind it, Fernando couldn't see anything.

He ran to the gate where the big trucks were thundering in and out.

"Move on, kid," called the guard. "You can't hang around here."

"I only wanted to watch," said Fernando. But he moved away from the gate. He walked slowly around the fence—looking, looking.

Suddenly he saw a break at the bottom of the fence. He got down on his hands and knees and peeked under. He grinned with happiness as he watched the machines.

Suddenly someone asked, "Could I try it?"

Fernando looked up. There stood a boy just about his own age. He started to say "Go away!" but he changed his mind.

"Sure," he said instead, and got up.

The boy got down and looked.

"Wow," he said, smiling, "this is great! This is really great!"

Fernando nodded his head as he waited his turn. But before it came, the guard appeared from the gate.

"You're not allowed here," said the guard angrily, as he pulled the boy to his feet. "Now go away!"

The boy turned and ran.

Fernando walked slowly around the fence, thinking all the time. How could he get to see over the top? Then he had the answer.

Great! he thought as he hurried to the supermarket. He found a discarded box and dragged it back to the fence.

He was just starting to climb when he felt someone looking at him. He turned around. There was that boy watching from the corner.

Fernando hesitated, then waved to him. "Want a look?" he called out.

The boy thought awhile. He looked up and down the street to see if the guard was coming. "Sure!" he said and climbed up.

Fernando waited and waited, but the boy gave no signs of coming down.

"Move over," said Fernando politely. "Make room for me."

But the boy did not hear him. He was too busy watching the machines.

"Hey, up there," Fernando called out, much louder this time. "MAKE ROOM FOR ME!"

Just then a loud whistle pierced the air.

"Come down!" shouted the guard, rounding the corner. "Do you want to fall off and break a leg?"

The boy climbed down swiftly, then ran. But he managed to give Fernando a hot angry look before he took off.

Fernando sat down with his back against the fence. He listened to the high sounds, the low sounds, the loud sounds, the soft sounds, the exciting sounds of the big machines until he felt he could stand it no longer. There was nothing he wanted more than to look over that fence.

Fernando searched the street—up and down. Then his eye fell on a streetlight pole.

There was that boy, halfway up that pole, looking with fascination at the machines.

"Could I have a look?" called Fernando.

The boy hesitated so long that Fernando almost gave up. Then the boy made up his mind. He reached down to help Fernando climb just as the guard came up.

"This has got to stop!" said the guard. "Why don't you watch through the holes in the fence like everyone else does?"

"There are no holes," said both boys together.

The guard clapped his hand to his head. "Don't tell me they forgot to drill the holes!" he groaned.

Sure enough, when the guard checked he found they had forgotten.

The guard went inside and got a big drill. He picked a good spot on the fence while both boys watched and waited.

As soon as he finished the first hole, both boys crowded in.

"Check it out!" said Fernando, his nose pressed against the fence. "This is great! This is really great!"

The other boy looked through the hole.

"Awesome!" he said, letting out a low whistle.

Fernando whistled, too. Just like his friend. Then both boys began to smile. But they never took their eyes off those magic machines.

THE SURPRISE SURPRISE PARTY

By Alan Cliburn

Danny was folding newspapers in the back yard when his mother appeared at the window. "The circulation manager just called," she said. "You have a cancellation—4879 Willis Street."

Danny frowned. "That's Mrs. Carter's house! Why do you think she's stopping the paper? She's been on my route ever since I started."

"I heard just this morning that she has moved to that large retirement home on Whitman Boulevard," his mother explained. "But I had forgotten that she was on your paper route."

"She's one of my favorite customers," Danny answered. He looked at his mother. "Why would she want to live in a retirement home? I thought those homes were only for people who couldn't walk or had had a bad stroke."

"No, not really," his mother said. "But it is for people who don't feel safe living alone anymore. Mrs. Carter will be eighty-five on her birthday next week, and she wanted to be where someone can keep an eye on her. She has fallen several times."

"I didn't know that," Danny said. "Well, I had better get started now." He loaded all the papers on his bike and rode out of the yard.

Danny had been delivering papers for so long that he didn't even look at the route book as he pedaled along.

When he came to 4879 Willis Street, Danny threw the paper onto the porch, same as always.

"She doesn't live there anymore," the lady next door told him.

"That's right!" Danny exclaimed, remembering.

He made a circle with his bike and rode back to get the paper.

"But she's paying for the whole month," the lady went on. "She left the money with me. Just a minute and I'll get it."

Danny smiled as he waited. It wasn't even the middle of the month, and she was paying for all of it. That was just like Mrs. Carter, all right. She was always doing nice things for people in the neighborhood.

Danny remembered one time when his mother was sick and couldn't have a birthday party for him. Somehow Mrs. Carter had found out and surprised him with a party, after all.

The last house on his route was about two blocks from Whitman Boulevard and the retirement home where Mrs. Carter had moved. Suddenly Danny had an idea. Mrs. Carter was paying for the paper. She might as well get it.

A few minutes later he was standing in the room Mrs. Carter shared with another woman.

"This is such a wonderful surprise, Danny!" Mrs. Carter began. "I can't ask you to bring my paper this far, though."

"It's not so far," Danny assured her. "Besides, you have it coming." He lowered his voice. "Do you like it here?"

Mrs. Carter nodded. "Yes, it's very nice, and everything is kept so clean." She smiled. "Of course I will miss seeing my friends from Willis Street—especially the children. You don't see many children in this home."

"I guess not," Danny said. "Well, I had better be going. I'll see you tomorrow."

He left the room and hurried down the hall. As he passed one room, he heard voices singing "Happy Birthday." The door was open, so Danny looked in.

A woman about the age of Mrs. Carter or even older sat in her bed, a small cake in front of her. The woman who shared the room and the nurse were the only other people there. It didn't look like much of a party to Danny.

As he was riding home on his bicycle, he remembered something his mother had said earlier: "Mrs. Carter will be eighty-five on her birthday next week."

Is that the kind of party she'll have? he thought. She deserved better, a lot better. At the party she had given for him there were balloons and streamers and presents—besides all his friends.

He was nearly home when he made the decision. Mrs. Carter would have the best birthday party she ever had! He would buy the decorations with his own money and ask his mother to bake the birthday cake. Would Mrs. Carter be surprised!

The next day he started inviting the boys and girls who lived on Willis Street. Mrs. Carter had taken care of most of them at one time or another and had always given them cookies and other treats on their birthdays.

"A party for Mrs. Carter?" Billy repeated, when Danny told him about it. "No, I don't have time."

"It's too far away," Susan told him. "Besides, I have my piano lesson that day."

"I can't," Scott replied. "Anyway, Mrs. Carter forgot *my* birthday last year!"

It was the same all over the neighborhood. "They sure forgot how nice she was to them," Danny said to his mother when he returned home. "That's all right," his mother said. "I'll still bake the best birthday cake you ever saw!"

Danny smiled. "Really? Then I'll still buy the streamers and balloons. It won't be a very big party, but it will be a good one—and Mrs. Carter will be surprised!"

On the afternoon of Mrs. Carter's birthday, Danny hurried home from school as fast as possible. "I'll deliver my papers and meet you at the home," he told his mother. "But how can we fix up the room for the surprise party if she's in it?"

"I talked to a nurse at the home this morning," his mother replied. "Mrs. Carter will be in the lounge, listening to a guest speaker for most of the afternoon. I'll put up the streamers while she's out, and you can help with the balloons."

Danny set a new record for speed on his paper route that day and arrived at the retirement home by 4:30. His mother was attaching the final streamer, when he entered Mrs. Carter's room.

"Boy, that looks nice!" Danny said. "But where are the balloons?"

In the closet," his mother said. Then she stopped talking. "Listen, Danny," she whispered. "I think I hear Mrs. Carter coming. Quickly hide behind the door."

A moment later Mrs. Carter and the woman who shared her room came through the doorway.

"My, wasn't that an interesting speaker?" Mrs. Carter began. "I—"

"Surprise!" Danny shouted, jumping out from behind the door.

"Happy Birthday!" his mother added.

Mrs. Carter looked up, a stunned expression on her face. Then she smiled. "Danny! Mrs. Reed! What a nice surprise!"

Suddenly the closet door opened. "Surprise!" several voices cried at the same time. "Happy Birthday!"

Danny's mouth dropped open as children from Willis Street came out of the closet, their arms full of balloons and presents.

"Wow, this *is* a surprise!" Danny exclaimed.

His mother smiled. "We thought it might be fun if the one who planned the surprise party was surprised, too."

"And this is the best birthday party I've ever had!" Mrs. Carter announced as she tried on a fancy party hat. "Thank you all for coming. And a special thanks to my very special friend—Danny."